Wuthering Heights

EMILY BRONTË
adapted by David Bennett

OXFORD
UNIVERSITY PRESS

1 ⬿ MR LOCKWOOD VISITS WUTHERING HEIGHTS

NOVEMBER 1801

The man on the other side of the large gate was tall and dark. He had the look of a gypsy. His eyes were almost black and his brows close together. There was no smile on his face. I looked past him to the house.

Wuthering Heights stood all alone, high up on the bleak* Yorkshire moors*. It was a lonely house. On one side of it there were a few fir trees, bent double by years of the north wind. The house was solid and strong, so that it could defend itself against the weather. The windows were narrow. Too narrow to let in any good light and too small for anyone to climb out. Around the door were lots of stone carvings, deformed* by the wind and rain. The name 'Hareton Earnshaw' was carved above the door and the date '1500'. It was a chilling place. Around the house, as far as the eye could see, was moorland.

I looked back to the man at the gate. 'Mr Heathcliff?' I asked. He nodded.

'I am Mr Lockwood, your new tenant* at Thrushcross Grange,' I said.

'Come,' he muttered without opening the gate. Only when my horse pushed against it, did he lead me up to the house.

'Joseph, take Mr Lockwood's horse away,' Heathcliff shouted. 'And bring us some wine.'

My horse was taken to the stables* by the servant. He was a grumpy-looking old man who muttered something under his breath as he left.

Heathcliff took me into the house, saying nothing. The inside

3

of the house was plain. It was the sort of house typical of many northern farmers. Heathcliff, however, looked out of place in it. He was an upright and handsome man with unusual features.

I sat down by the fire in the sitting-room. We were waiting for the wine. Heathcliff was silent. Three dogs sat at my feet. I started to stroke one of them. It growled.

'Better leave her alone,' muttered Heathcliff. 'She's not kept as a pet,' he added, standing up and walking to the door.

'Joseph, where's that wine?' he shouted.

Joseph's mumbled reply, whatever it was, was not good enough. Heathcliff set off for the cellar*, leaving me in the room with the three dogs. I made faces at the dogs, and suddenly one of them leapt at me. I put my hands up and flung her away. The other dogs started barking. This brought even more dogs out from their hiding places. I shouted for help.

Heathcliff and Joseph came slowly up from the cellar. They did not rush to help me. Luckily, the housekeeper* ran from the kitchen into the sitting-room. She was shouting at the top of her voice and waving a frying pan around her head. The dogs let go.

'What's the matter?' demanded Heathcliff, coming into the room.

'What's the matter?' I said. 'You might as well have left me in your house with tigers.'

'They won't go for people who touch nothing,' he replied, his eyes full of anger.

Then his mood changed and, smiling, he added, 'Will you have a drink with me?'

'No thank you,' I snapped back.

'Oh come on, Mr Lockwood,' said Heathcliff, still smiling. 'You aren't hurt, are you?'

I did not want him to laugh at me any more, so I took the drink. Heathcliff began to relax and told me all about my new home, Thrushcross Grange. I enjoyed listening to him so much that I suggested I might return tomorrow. Heathcliff wanted no such thing, but I knew I would return anyway. I was so taken both by* him and by Wuthering Heights.

2 ∾ MR LOCKWOOD MEETS CATHY AND HARETON

The next day was cold and misty. Even so, I walked the four miles to Wuthering Heights. The air was freezing and the ground covered in frost. By the time I arrived, it was snowing. I ran to the front door and banged hard on it. The dogs howled but no one answered. I banged again. I needed to get out of the cold.

'What do you want?'

I looked round to see Joseph's head poking out of a window in the barn.

'Master's in t'field*,' he said.

'Is there nobody in the house?' I asked.

'Only t'missis*, and she'll not let thee in,' Joseph added as his head disappeared.

The snow was getting worse. I grabbed the handle of the door and shook it. Just then, a young man shouted for me to follow him. He took me to the back door and let me in. I was pleased to see not only a roaring fire but also 't'missis'.

'Rough weather, Mrs Heathcliff,' I said.

She did not answer. We sat in silence for several minutes.

Finally she spoke. 'You should not have come out in such weather,' she said, getting up.

I could see her more clearly now. She was very young and slim, with golden curly hair and sad eyes.

I turned to the young man who had led me indoors. He was staring at me. He did not look or sound like a servant. His dress and speech were both simple. His hair was thick and untidy and his hands were rough. My thoughts were stopped by Heathcliff.

'Are you mad coming out in this?' he snapped, as he walked into the room. 'Even local people can get lost on the moors in this weather.' Then, turning to Mrs Heathcliff, he shouted, 'Get the tea ready!'

He was so rude I could not believe it.

'You must be very happy out here with your good lady,' I said, changing the subject.

'My good lady?' he asked.

'Mrs Heathcliff, your wife,' I said, looking at the lady.

'My wife is dead. This, this is my daughter-in-law,' he said, looking at her with hatred.

I felt awful. I looked back to the young man who had led me inside. He must be her husband, I thought. Again I was wrong.

'My daughter-in-law's husband is dead,' said Heathcliff, reading my thoughts.

'And this young man?' I asked.

'Hareton Earnshaw,' the young man growled, staring at me.

I looked outside. It was dark and snowing heavily. I was worried about getting home and said so. No one took any notice. I tried again.

'Mrs Heathcliff,' I said, 'how am I to get home?'

'The same way you came,' she replied. 'But there is no one to guide you.'

'Then I must stay,' I said.

'You will share a bed with Hareton or Joseph if you do. I do not trust any stranger to be left alone in my house,' said Heathcliff.

I was very angry at this. How dare he not trust me? I ran past him and out into the yard. It was so dark that I could not see. I grabbed a lamp from Joseph and ran to the gate. I heard the dogs chasing after me. Two of them knocked me to the ground. I shouted for them to get off me. I could hear Heathcliff laughing. I was saved once again by the housekeeper, Zillah. She ran out, screaming at the dogs. They let go of me and Zillah took me back inside.

I felt sick, dizzy, and faint. I now had no choice but to stay for the night.

3 ∾ CATHERINE'S GHOST

Zillah led me upstairs and into a small room. It had little in it: a small chair, a clothes press*, and next to the window a large oak bed. The bed had curtains around it to hide the sleeper from anyone else in the room.

'The master does not like anybody to use this room,' said Zillah.

'Why not?' I asked.

'I don't know,' she said. 'I have worked here two years and there have been many strange goings on in this house.'

I was too unwell to worry about 'strange goings on'. Zillah left me alone. I walked across to the large oak bed. I placed my candle on the window ledge and shut the curtains behind me. The candle lit up the corner of the ledge. It had three names written all over it – *Catherine Earnshaw, Catherine Heathcliff,* and *Catherine Linton.*

Then I noticed some books which had belonged to Catherine. She had written stories all over them about herself and Heathcliff. They had been very close. I read for a while. Then I fell asleep and had the most terrible dream.

In my dream, the wind outside was fierce. The branch of a fir tree was knocking against the window. I got up to stop it but the window was shut tight. I couldn't move it. The knocking of the branch was getting worse. I smashed the window with my hand and reached through to grab the branch. My fingers closed on an ice-cold hand! Terrified*, I tried to pull my arm away, but the hand clung on.

'Let me in! Let me in!' a voice said.

'Who are you?' I asked, shaking.

'Catherine Linton,' the voice replied. 'I was lost on the moor but now I have found my way home.'

As she spoke, I could see a child's face through the window. I was terrified. I tried again to pull my hand away. The grip tightened. I pulled the child's wrist onto the broken glass and rubbed it backwards and forwards. Blood ran down and soaked the bedclothes.

'Let me in!' the voice wailed*.

'Let me go, if you want me to let you in.'

The fingers let go. I pulled my hand through the glass and piled some books up in front of the window.

8

The voice wailed again, 'Let me in!'

'Never!' I shouted. 'Not if you cry for twenty years.'

'It has been twenty years,' said the voice. 'I have been out here for twenty years.' The hand scratched at the books, which began to move. I tried to get away but fear froze me to the spot. I cried out.

The bedroom door opened and Heathcliff came in. I could see him through the curtains of the bed. He looked around.

'At last,' he whispered, then added, 'Is anyone here?' He clearly was not expecting an answer.

I opened the curtains. Heathcliff stood in his shirt and trousers, looking as white as the wall behind him. The candle he held was dripping wax over his fingers.

'It is only your guest, sir,' I called out.

'Who showed you up to this room?' he said. 'Who was it?' He was so angry that he was grinding his teeth* and crushing his nails into his palms.

'It was Zillah,' I said. 'She told me about the strange goings on in this house. Well, I can tell you it is swarming with ghosts,' I added. Then I started to tell him about my dream.

When I mentioned the name Catherine, Heathcliff sent me out of the room.

I stood out of his sight and watched as he got onto the bed. He wrenched* open the window. Then, sobbing, he shouted, 'Come in! Come in, Cathy, do come. Oh do, once more. Oh! My heart's darling, hear me this time – Cathy, at last!'

The ghost did not show itself. The snow and wind drove through the window, blowing out the candle.

I could not stay any longer in that house. I went downstairs and waited in the kitchen. At first light*, I set off for Thrushcross Grange. I arrived four hours later, ill but safe.

4 ❧ HEATHCLIFF COMES TO WUTHERING HEIGHTS

It was dusk when Mrs Nelly Dean, my housekeeper, brought supper in. I was still weak but wanted to find out more about Wuthering Heights.

'Why does Heathcliff let* Thrushcross Grange and choose to live at Wuthering Heights?' I asked.

'He is very rich, sir,' she said, 'and yet very greedy. By letting Thrushcross Grange he gets more money.'

'I heard he had a son.'

'Yes, but he died.'

'And Mrs Heathcliff is the widow*?'

'Yes.'

'Where did she come from?'

'She is my late master's daughter. Catherine Linton is her name.'

Catherine Linton! That was one of the names written on the window ledge.

'And who is that Earnshaw, Hareton Earnshaw who lives with Mr Heathcliff?' I asked.

'He is the young lady's cousin, the late Mrs Linton's nephew.'

It was all rather confusing. 'Mrs Dean,' I said, 'will you tell me more about my neighbours at Wuthering Heights?'

'Indeed I will, sir,' she said. 'Just let me get my sewing.'

A short while later, she returned and began to tell her story. It started in 1771.

Thirty years ago I spent a lot of time at Wuthering Heights. Mr Earnshaw, my mother's old master, had two children, Hindley and Catherine. I played with them often. One day, when

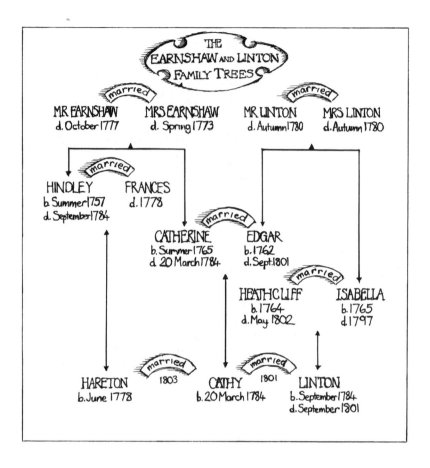

THE EARNSHAW AND LINTON FAMILY TREES

MR EARNSHAW
d. October 1777
married
MRS EARNSHAW
d. Spring 1773

MR LINTON
d. Autumn 1780
married
MRS LINTON
d. Autumn 1780

HINDLEY
b. Summer 1757
d. September 1784
married
FRANCES
d. 1778

CATHERINE
b. Summer 1765
d. 20 March 1784
married
EDGAR
b. 1762
d. Sept. 1801

HEATHCLIFF
b. 1764
d. May 1802
married
ISABELLA
b. 1765
d. 1797

HARETON
b. June 1778
married 1803
CATHY
b. 20 March 1784
married 1801
LINTON
b. September 1784
d. September 1801

Hindley was fourteen and Catherine just six, Mr Earnshaw decided to go to Liverpool. It was a decision that was to change all our lives.

Mr Earnshaw came back from Liverpool with a small child. He was a dirty, ragged*, black-haired boy that he had rescued off the streets. He had brought him back to live at Wuthering Heights. Mrs Earnshaw was very angry. Hindley wanted nothing to do with the boy. Neither did Catherine at first. However, Heathcliff, as they named him, and Catherine soon became very close.

Over the next two years, Catherine and Heathcliff grew closer whilst Hindley and Heathcliff grew further apart. Hindley would often beat Heathcliff, but the boy would never cry or tell on Hindley. He suffered in silence. When Mrs Earnshaw died, Hindley lost not only his mother but also his only friend. He was jealous of Heathcliff, who was his father's favourite. A hatred grew between Hindley and Heathcliff that was to last a lifetime.

5 ∾ HINDLEY IS SENT AWAY

Mr Earnshaw had always been fit and healthy. However, soon after his wife died, he too became ill. As he grew ill, so he became bad tempered. He would not hear anything said against Heathcliff. Hindley, of course, could not hide his hatred for his 'brother'. Mr Earnshaw became even more angry with him.

Hindley was sent away to college and I hoped the house would become peaceful. Joseph and Catherine stopped this happening. You will have met Joseph, the servant at Wuthering Heights. He was, and still is, a most horrible man and yet he had a huge effect on old Mr Earnshaw. He would tell tales to him about all the children, always making it clear that Catherine and Hindley were the worst.

Catherine was a law unto herself. She had beautiful eyes and the sweetest smile. But she was much too fond of Heathcliff. The worst thing anybody could do to her was to keep her away from him. From the moment she got up until the time she went to bed, she was nothing but trouble.

One October evening, the old man was sitting in his chair. Catherine had been sick during the day and she was, for once, still. As she sat next to her father, with Heathcliff's head on her lap, her father said to her, 'Why can't you always be a good lass*, Catherine?'

She replied, 'Why can't you always be a good man, father?'

She saw she had upset him, so she kissed his hand and began to sing him to sleep. A sleep from which he never woke up.

6 ∾ CATHERINE AND HEATHCLIFF VISIT THRUSHCROSS GRANGE

Mr Hindley came home for his father's funeral, bringing with him a wife, Frances. She was young and thin and had eyes as bright as diamonds. Who she was and where she came from we were never told. She had neither money nor name*.

Mr Hindley had changed a lot during his three years away. He spoke and dressed quite differently. He was thinner and had lost his colour, but now he was master of the house. He could treat Heathcliff how he liked. Mr Hindley told Joseph and me that we had to live in the back kitchen. The rest of the house was to be only for Frances, Catherine, and himself.

Catherine and Heathcliff were treated very differently. At first, Frances bought Catherine presents and played with her. However, she soon tired of being kind, and when she decided that she disliked Heathcliff, he was sent to work in the fields. Often, he and Catherine would run away for the day to the moors. When they came back, they were punished. It made no difference. When they were together, they did not care about anybody else.

One Sunday evening, the two of them were still missing at bedtime. I was told by Mr Hindley to lock all the doors and not let them in. I went to bed but could not sleep. I watched for them from my window. It was pouring with rain. After a while, I saw a lantern* coming up the road. It was Heathcliff, but there was no Catherine. I ran downstairs and let him in.

'Where is Catherine?' I said. 'Is she hurt?'

'At Thrushcross Grange,' Heathcliff replied. 'I would have been there too but they threw me out.'

'What were you doing at Thrushcross Grange?'

'Catherine and I went to see if the Linton children are treated as badly as us.'

'Probably not,' I said. 'They are good children, unlike you two.'

'Nonsense, Nelly. Let me tell you what we saw,' he said angrily.

'What?' I replied.

'We looked through the window into this large room. The children, Edgar and Isabella, were all alone. They should have been happy. Catherine and I would have been.'

'What were they doing?' I asked.

'Isabella, who is eleven, a year younger than Catherine, lay screaming on the floor. Edgar stood by the fire, crying. They were arguing over who should hold the dog. Can you believe it? You would never find Catherine and me arguing like that. If she wanted something, I would give it to her and she to me.'

His voice was full of anger. I told him to keep it down or Mr Hindley would hear. 'You haven't told me why Catherine is not with you,' I said.

'We were laughing at those silly Linton children and they heard us. They ran to the door and shouted to their parents. We heard the door opening, so we ran. They let the dogs loose. One grabbed Catherine's foot and pulled her to the ground and she fainted. I could not leave her. We were both taken back to the house.'

'Then what happened?' I asked.

'We were taken into the living room as thieves. Mrs Linton

looked at me and raised her hands in horror. Edgar and Isabella crept closer for a better look. While they were looking at me, Catherine came round. Edgar looked at her.

'"That's Miss Earnshaw," he said. "I have seen her in church."

'"Miss Earnshaw? Nonsense," said Mrs Linton. "She would not mix with a gypsy."

'"That is the strange boy the late Mr Earnshaw brought back from Liverpool a few years ago," said Mr Linton.

'"He is a wicked* boy and not fit to be in this house," said Mrs Linton.

'This made me so angry, Nelly, that I started swearing. I was pushed out of the house with a lantern in my hand and told to go home. I didn't. Instead, I crept back to see if Catherine was safe. She was sitting on the sofa with the Lintons fussing around her. They were bathing her wound, giving her cakes, and combing her hair. You could see that they admired* her. She is so superior to* them – to everybody – is she not, Nelly?'

I did not answer other than to say that Mr Hindley would be very angry when he found out. My words came true. Mr Hindley did not flog* Heathcliff. Instead he gave him the worst punishment possible. He told Heathcliff he must never speak to Catherine again. If he did, he would be sent away from Wuthering Heights.

7 ∾ HINDLEY TREATS HEATHCLIFF BADLY

Catherine stayed at Thrushcross Grange for five weeks. Frances visited her often, taking her fine clothes and flattering* her. It was all part of the plan to keep Catherine and Heathcliff apart.

Catherine returned to Wuthering Heights a different person. She was no longer a wild, hatless little savage but a finely-dressed young woman. I remember the day she returned home. She came

17

into the kitchen, gave me a hug, and then asked, 'Where's Heathcliff?'

Mr Hindley answered, 'Heathcliff, you may come forward.'

Heathcliff came slowly out from behind a bench. He had been in the fields all day. He looked untidy and dirty. Catherine did not mind. She ran and hugged him, giving him several kisses. Suddenly she let go, looked at him, and burst out laughing.

'You look very black* and cross,' she said, 'but that's because I am used to Edgar and Isabella Linton. They are always so clean. Have you forgotten me, Heathcliff?'

'Shake hands, Heathcliff,' said Mr Hindley.

'I shall not,' he replied. 'I shall not be laughed at.'

'I did not mean to laugh at you,' Catherine said. 'Shake hands at least. Why are you sulking? I only laughed because you look so odd. If you washed your face and brushed your hair, you would be all right. You look so dirty!'

'You needn't have touched me,' he answered. 'I shall be as dirty as I want. I like to be dirty.'

He was so angry he ran out of the room. Catherine was upset, but Mr Hindley and Frances just laughed.

The next day was Christmas Day. The Lintons had been invited to Wuthering Heights. They had accepted* but Edgar and Isabella were to be kept away from the 'naughty screaming boy'.

When they were all at church, Heathcliff came into the kitchen.

'Nelly, make me decent. I'm going to be good,' he said.

'About time, Heathcliff,' I said. 'You have upset Catherine enough. She is sorry she ever came home.'

'Did she say that?' he asked.

'She cried when I told her you were on the moors again this morning.'

'Well, I cried last night,' he said.

'There is no need to be jealous of* Edgar Linton,' I said.

'I wish I had light hair and fair skin like him. I wish I was well dressed and well behaved and as rich as him.'

'Oh, Heathcliff,' I said, 'you are younger than Edgar, yet you are taller, twice as broad* across the shoulders, and far more a man than him.'

I think he felt better at that. I wanted to say more but the sound of a coach made me stop. The Earnshaws and Lintons were back from church. Heathcliff went to meet them but he had not left the kitchen when Mr Hindley saw him. Wanting to keep his promise to the Lintons, he told me to send the boy to his room until dinner was over. 'Be gone, you rascal*,' he shouted at Heathcliff, 'before I pull your hair and make it longer!'

'It's long enough,' said Edgar Linton, who was now in the room. 'I am surprised he can see.'

At this remark, Heathcliff lost his temper. He picked up a

dish of hot apple sauce off the table and threw it into Edgar's face. Edgar screamed so loudly that Catherine and Isabella came running in to see what was going on.

Mr Hindley grabbed Heathcliff and took him upstairs. Catherine turned to Edgar. 'You should not have spoken to him like that. Now he will be flogged. I hate to see him flogged.'

'I didn't speak *to* him, I spoke *about* him,' said Edgar.

At this point Mr Hindley came back rubbing his hands. 'Now I've seen to him, let's have some dinner,' he said.

The Earnshaws and the Lintons sat down to dinner. Catherine was upset and did not eat much. After dinner we sang carols. Catherine left the room, saying that they sounded better from the top of the stairs. Later, when I went to find her, she was in Heathcliff's room. I was afraid of what might happen if Hindley found out, so I took them both downstairs. I made Heathcliff some food but he was not hungry.

'What's the matter?' I asked.

'I am thinking how I can get my revenge* on Hindley,' he said. 'I don't care how long I have to wait. I just hope he will not die before me.'

At this Mrs Dean stood up. 'It is late, Mr Lockwood,' she said, 'and I must go to bed.'

I told her she would do no such thing, as I wanted to hear more of her story.

'In that case, Mr Lockwood, sir, let me move forward a few months to the summer of 1778.'

8 ∾ EDGAR FALLS IN LOVE

It was a fine June day when Hareton Earnshaw was born. The baby was healthy but Frances was very ill. I heard the doctor tell

Mr Hindley, 'She will be dead before winter.' I knew that I would have to look after the baby when she died. Mr Hindley had room in his heart only for two people – Frances and himself. And so it was. Frances died early that winter and I was left to look after Hareton.

Mr Hindley became worse. Every night he drank himself to sleep. All the servants left except Joseph and me. Joseph stayed to show the master that he could not ignore God and survive. He was always quoting the Bible at him and seemed to like telling Mr Hindley what would happen if he turned his back on God. I stayed on to look after little Hareton and Catherine. During this time Mr Hindley treated Heathcliff terribly, but the boy rarely* complained. He was happy watching Mr Hindley drink himself slowly to death.

Catherine was fifteen now and truly beautiful. She was still headstrong* and, I confess, I did not like her very much. She remained close to Heathcliff, and Edgar Linton found it hard to make the same impression. She was a clever girl too. On her regular visits to Thrushcross Grange, she was amusing, polite, and intelligent. She was careful to show her good side. At Wuthering Heights she was the opposite, behaving badly all the time. Yet there was a hint of weakness about her.

Heathcliff spent most of his time working in the fields. He was sixteen and always in a black mood* . He made no effort to keep himself clean and tidy. In fact, he seemed to want people to dislike him. Catherine still spent time with him when he was not working, but he found it hard to accept affection* from her.

One day Mr Hindley went into town, so Heathcliff decided he would take the day off. He came to the house and asked Catherine if she was busy that afternoon.

'No,' she said.

It was a lie. She had arranged for Edgar to come and see her.

'So why are you wearing that silk frock*?' he said. 'Nobody's coming here, I hope?'

'Not that I know of,' she lied again.

Catherine tried to get Heathcliff to go back to the fields, but he refused. They fell silent. Finally, Catherine said, 'Isabella and Edgar Linton said they might call this afternoon. If they do, it would be better for you not to be here.'

'Tell Nelly to say you are busy,' he said. 'You spend far too much time with them anyway.'

'Why shouldn't I?' she said. 'You are no company. You never say anything to amuse me.'

'You never told me before that you dislike my company.'

'It is no company at all when people know nothing and say nothing,' she snapped.

Heathcliff stood up to say something. As he did so, Edgar Linton came into the room smiling.

'Am I too early?' he said, as Heathcliff went out.

'No,' answered Catherine. Then she turned to me and asked what I was doing in the room.

'I have to get my work done, Miss,' I said. Actually, Mr Hindley had told me not to leave her alone with Edgar Linton.

She walked across the room and whispered, 'Go away.' She pinched my arm as she did so.

'Ow!' I screamed. 'Why did you pinch me, Miss?'

'I didn't touch you, you liar!' she shouted.

'What's that then?' I said, showing her and Edgar the mark on my arm.

She lifted her arm and slapped me across the face.

'Catherine love, Catherine,' said Edgar. He was clearly shocked.

Hareton started crying and shouted, 'Wicked Aunt Catherine!' She grabbed hold of the boy and shook him. Edgar

could not believe that the woman he loved could do such a thing. He grabbed Hareton and gave him to me. He got a slap across the face for his efforts. Then he picked up his hat and walked towards the door.

'Where are you going?' demanded Catherine. 'You must not go.'

'I must and I shall,' he said. 'How can I stay after you lied to me and hit me?'

'I didn't,' she cried. 'Oh, go then if you want. Go and I'll cry myself sick,' she added, dropping to her knees and starting to cry.

Edgar walked out into the courtyard* but he could not resist* one last look. On seeing Catherine's tearful face at the window, he came back into the house. A little while later, I went to tell them of Mr Hindley's return. I could see that their quarrel* had brought them much closer together.

9 ∾ HEATHCLIFF LEAVES AND CATHERINE MARRIES EDGAR

Mr Hindley was very drunk when he arrived back at Wuthering Heights. I was scared he might harm Hareton. I picked him up to hide him in a cupboard, but it was too late.

'You keep my son in a cupboard, do you?' he said, picking up a knife. 'I'll make you swallow this, Nelly.' He put the knife between my teeth. I knew he would not hurt me so I pushed the knife away. He turned and picked up Hareton. 'This is not my son,' he said, looking at him. 'My son would come running to greet me, not scream at me.' Poor Hareton was kicking and crying in his father's arms. Mr Hindley carried him upstairs and held him over the banister*. I ran after him. At that moment, Heathcliff entered the house.

'Who is that?' asked Mr Hindley, leaning over the banister. I

watched in horror as Hareton fell from his grip towards the floor below. Thankfully, Heathcliff caught him.

Heathcliff stared at the child and then looked up at Hindley. He did not need to say anything. His face said it all. He had just saved the life of his enemy's son, the man he had sworn to get revenge on. I ran downstairs and took Hareton into my arms. Almost at once, he stopped crying, but when his father tried to touch him, he cried louder than ever.

'You have him, Nelly,' he said as he reached for the brandy bottle.

'Please, Mr Hindley, no more,' I pleaded, but he took no notice. I went into the kitchen and Heathcliff walked towards the barn*. A few minutes later Catherine came in.

'Are you alone, Nelly?'

'Yes, Miss,' I replied.

She looked upset.

'Where's Heathcliff?' she asked.

'In the barn,' I said.

There was a silence. I could hear her crying.

'Nelly, will you keep a secret for me?' she asked.

'If it's worth keeping,' I said.

'Listen,' she said. 'Today Edgar Linton asked me to marry him and I have given him my answer. But before I tell you if I said yes or no, I want to know what you think.'

'He must be a fool to ask you after the way you treated him this afternoon,' I said.

She did not hear me.

'I said yes,' she said.

'What do you love about him?' I asked.

'He is handsome and pleasant to be with.'

'Bad,' I replied.

'He is young and cheerful,' she added.

'Even worse.'

'And he loves me.'

'That's worse still.'

'And he will be rich and I will be an important lady.'

'Worst of all. There are many other rich, handsome men in the world. Why don't you marry one of them?'

'I don't know any other rich, handsome men, only Edgar.'

'Well, I don't know why you are unhappy then, Miss Catherine. Mr Hindley will be pleased. Mr and Mrs Linton will be happy. You will leave this house for a richer one. You love Edgar and he loves you. What's the problem?'

'Here! And here!' replied Catherine, hitting her head and breast. 'In my heart and soul I know I'm wrong, but Hindley has made Heathcliff poor. It would degrade me* to marry him now...'

Before she had finished, I saw a movement outside. Heathcliff got up from the bench by the window and walked away. He had not been in the barn as I had thought. He had been listening.

'...so he will never know how I love him. That I love him with my soul. He is more myself than I am. Our souls are the same.'

'Quiet, Miss Catherine,' I said. I knew it was too late. 'Joseph is on his way back and Heathcliff may well be with him. How do you think Heathcliff will feel when you marry Edgar? He will be left all alone.'

'Left alone?' Catherine said. 'Left alone? I do not intend to leave him alone. When I marry Edgar, I will be able to use his money to help Heathcliff. Edgar must learn to accept him as my friend. If I married Heathcliff, we would both always be poor, but not this way.'

'That's the worst reason you have given yet for marrying Edgar,' I said.

'It is not. It is the best,' she replied. 'My love for Heathcliff is as strong as the eternal* rocks beneath the earth. My love for Edgar is like the leaves on the trees. Nelly, I am Heathcliff. He is always, always in my mind.'

'Don't ask me to keep any more of your secrets,' I said angrily.

'But you will keep that secret?' she asked.

'I'll not promise,' I replied.

At that moment Joseph came in. It was not until later that I told Catherine that I thought Heathcliff had heard us talking. She jumped up and ran out of the house, shouting his name. There was no sign of him.

It was a very dark evening for summer and it looked like thunder. I asked Catherine to come back inside but she took no notice. At midnight, the storm came sweeping across the moors towards Wuthering Heights. The wind lashed against the house and a huge branch smashed against the chimney, crashing it onto the roof. The storm passed in twenty minutes. Catherine had stayed outside, hoping Heathcliff would return. He did not. When the storm was over she came back inside, but it had given her a fever.

For several weeks she was not allowed out of bed. During that time Mrs Linton paid many visits and insisted Catherine finish her recovery at Thrushcross Grange. It was an act of kindness that was to kill both Mrs Linton and her husband, for they both caught the fever and died within a few days of each other.

Catherine got better, but the doctor said that if she fell ill again it could kill her too. Edgar Linton was still in love with her. Three years after his parents died she married him and moved to Thrushcross Grange. She insisted that I went with her. I had no choice, but it was with a heavy heart that I left little Hareton with his father. And Heathcliff? He had not been heard of since the night of the storm.

At this point, Mrs Dean looked at the clock. It was half past one in the morning. She was too tired to tell me any more and she went to bed. I stayed up for the next two hours, thinking about her strange tale.

10 ∾ ISABELLA FALLS FOR HEATHCLIFF

The next day, Mrs Dean told me more.

Miss Catherine behaved much better at Thrushcross Grange. She was kind to Mr Edgar and even showed fondness* to Isabella, his sister. Mr Edgar seemed scared of upsetting Catherine. Sometimes, when I was short* with her, he would frown at me. For six months all was well. Then, one September evening, everything changed.

I was coming in from the garden when I heard a voice behind me saying, 'Nelly, is that you?' It was a deep voice with a strange accent. I turned to look at the man in the porch. He was tall and dark and wearing dark clothes.

'I have waited for an hour,' he said, not showing his face. When a ray of light fell on him, I could see his cheeks. They were half covered in black whiskers and his eyes were deep set. It was the eyes I recognized.

'Is it really you?'

'Yes, it's me, Heathcliff,' he replied.

'What?' I said. 'You've come back after three years. How will my mistress take it?'

'I must see her,' he said. 'Tell her what you like but I must see her.'

'I'm not sure she should see you, sir. The shock would be too much.'

'Go, Nelly,' he said impatiently*.

Catherine and Mr Edgar were in the sitting-room. I hesitated* and then said, 'A person from the village wishes to see you, ma'am.'

'Very well,' she said. 'You may bring the tea up, Nelly. I will be back soon.'

'Who is it?' Mr Edgar asked.

'It's Heathcliff, sir. He used to live at Wuthering Heights.'

'What! That gypsy! Why did you not tell Catherine it was him?'

Before I had time to reply, Mr Edgar leaned out of the window and shouted: 'Don't stand outside in the cold. Bring him in, Catherine.'

Catherine ran upstairs and flung her arms around Mr Edgar. 'Oh Edgar, darling. It's Heathcliff. He's back. After all this time he's come back to see me.'

Mr Edgar was angry and showed it.

'Oh, Edgar! I know you don't like him but please, for my sake, be friends with him. Can I tell him to come up?' she pleaded.

'Not here in the sitting-room. I'll see him in the kitchen,' he said.

Catherine, as usual, got her own way and Heathcliff was brought into the sitting-room. I was amazed at how he had changed. He was tall and upright, a proper gentleman. The black fire still burned in his eyes. Mr Edgar tried to be polite but it was hard for him. He had to watch Catherine hang on Heathcliff's every word. Finally, much to Mr Edgar's annoyance, she took Heathcliff's hand and said, 'This is like a dream. How could you leave me for so long and never think of me?'

'I have thought more of you than you have of me,' he replied. 'I heard that you had married. Catherine, I came to see you just one more time and then take my revenge on Hindley. But your welcome has changed my mind. It has been hard since I left. I have struggled on only because of you.'

'Catherine, come and pour the tea before it gets cold,' said Mr Edgar. He was unable to hide his anger at what he was hearing.

'Where are you staying tonight, Mr Heathcliff?' I asked.

'Wuthering Heights,' he replied. 'Mr Hindley Earnshaw asked me to stay when I called this morning.'

This worried me. Why would Heathcliff want to stay with Mr Hindley when he hated him so much? Later that night, when Catherine came to see me, I asked her if she knew the answer.

'He went there to look for me,' she said. 'Hindley invited him to play cards and lost. So he wants to try and get his money back tonight. You know how greedy Hindley is.'

'Don't you fear for Heathcliff's safety?' I asked.

'Oh no, Nelly. He can look after himself,' she added.

Over the next few days, Heathcliff visited us regularly. Catherine was so sweet to Mr Edgar that he did not seem to mind. At first Heathcliff stayed only a short while, but soon he was stopping much longer. Then something astonishing happened.

One day, Isabella, who was now eighteen, told us that she found Heathcliff most attractive and that she was always thinking about him. Mr Edgar could not believe it. He knew that if he and Catherine did not have a son, then Isabella would inherit the Linton money. The thought of Heathcliff gaining this money was too much. Mr Edgar was sure that Heathcliff was plotting* something, but he did not know what.

Catherine and I tried to tell Isabella she was wrong to love Heathcliff. It made no difference.

I had heard of how Heathcliff was living at Wuthering Heights. Each night he and Hindley would drink and play cards.

Mr Hindley was losing heavily. Joseph had told me that Hindley borrowed money on his land* to pay Heathcliff. Despite what he was doing to Hindley, Isabella would hear nothing against Heathcliff. He made it clear that he had no desire for Isabella and yet I was troubled. I had heard him say to Catherine, 'Isabella will inherit the family wealth from Edgar, won't she?'

'If I have no sons,' she replied. 'But don't think about that, Heathcliff. Edgar and I will have plenty of sons.'

They never spoke of it again. Yet I could see Heathcliff thought about it often.

Over the next few days, I watched him closely. His visits were like a nightmare. How I wished he had never returned. I was worried about Mr Hindley and Hareton. They were like lost sheep about to be pounced on by an evil beast.

11 ∾ MR EDGAR AND HEATHCLIFF FIGHT

I knew I had to go to Wuthering Heights to warn Mr Hindley of the danger from Heathcliff. One bright frosty afternoon, I set off. The closer I got to the house, the more worried I became. Hareton stood at the gate. He had not changed much in the ten months since I had left.

'Hareton, it's me – Nelly,' I said.

He picked up a large stone and threw it at me. The stone hit my bonnet* and the boy swore at me.

'Who taught you such words?' I asked.

'Heathcliff,' he said.

I told him to go to the house and tell his father that Nelly Dean was waiting for him at the gate, but Heathcliff opened the door and on seeing him I ran away.

The next time Heathcliff came to Thrushcross Grange, I saw him kiss Isabella.

'You traitor!' I shouted from the kitchen.

'What is it, Nelly?' asked Catherine. She had just come in.

'It's Heathcliff,' I said. 'I've just seen him kissing Miss Isabella.'

'I will deal with this, Nelly,' she said. 'What are you doing, Heathcliff? If you do not leave Isabella alone, Edgar will stop you coming.'

'Let him try!' Heathcliff shouted. 'I am not afraid of him. What does it matter to you anyway? I am not your husband. Why are you jealous of me?'

'I am not jealous of you, I am jealous for you. If you want to marry Isabella, then do so. But do you like her? I am sure you don't.'

I could listen no more and went to find Mr Edgar. I told him what had happened. He came downstairs, told the servants to wait in the passage, and went into the kitchen.

'I have had enough of your visits, Heathcliff,' he said. 'You are no longer welcome in this house. If you have not gone in three minutes, I will have you thrown out.'

Heathcliff looked at Mr Edgar. 'Cathy, this lamb of yours threatens like a bull!' he said.

Mr Edgar waved to me to get the servants but Catherine reached the door first and locked it.

'You must fight man to man,' she said to her husband.

Mr Edgar tried to grab the door key off her, but she threw it on the fire. Mr Edgar went pale, trembled, covered his face with his hands, and slumped into a chair.

'And you prefer him to me?' said Heathcliff, walking across to Mr Edgar and pushing the chair. Mr Edgar jumped up and punched him in the throat. Heathcliff fell back and Mr Edgar walked out of the back door and into the garden.

'Now you'll never be able to come here again,' said Catherine. 'He will come back with men and guns. Go quickly.'

Heathcliff smashed the lock off the door and left just as Mr Edgar returned with his men.

Catherine told me to go upstairs with her. She was angry at what Mr Edgar had done to Heathcliff and wanted to talk. 'If Edgar will not let me keep Heathcliff for my friend, I will break both their hearts by breaking my own,' she told me.

Mr Edgar followed us to the parlour. 'Catherine,' he said, 'you must choose between me and Heathcliff. Who will it be?'

'Leave me alone. I am ill!' she shouted. 'Can't you see I can hardly stand? Edgar, leave me!'

She fell onto the floor. Mr Edgar looked horrified.

'There is nothing the matter with her,' I whispered to him. 'She told me she was going to pretend to be ill to scare you.'

Catherine heard me. She ran into her bedroom, locked the door, and did not come out.

12 ∾ CATHERINE DECLARES HER LOVE FOR HEATHCLIFF

It was three days later when Catherine's door opened. She asked for something to eat and drink. During that time, Mr Edgar had read his books and Isabella had cried for Heathcliff. I was not worried for I thought Catherine was acting. How wrong I was.

'What is Edgar doing?' she demanded.

'He is well and reading,' I said.

'He is reading his books when I am dying? How dare he!' she screamed.

She picked up her pillow and ripped it open with her teeth. She began to ramble*. She talked of Heathcliff and of birds and of all sorts of things. It reminded me of her illness the night Heathcliff left Wuthering Heights. Suddenly, she looked into the mirror and screamed, 'Do you see that face?'

'That is your face,' I said.

'No, no, Nelly, the room is haunted,' she cried. 'I am frightened of being alone. I wish I was back at Wuthering Heights in my bed with the wind blowing through the trees. Open the window, Nelly, and let me feel the wind from the moors.'

I did as she asked but I was troubled. She had a fever. Now she lay still, tears rolling down her face. 'I wish I was a child again, young and free on the moors with Heathcliff. I felt so happy then. Open the window, Nelly – wider this time.'

'I can't,' I said. 'I don't want you to die of cold.'

'You won't give me a chance of life, you mean,' she said. She jumped out of bed and opened the window. The cold air came rushing into the room. Catherine did not move. Outside it was black. There was no moon and no lights from any other houses.

'Look!' she shouted, looking into the darkness. 'There's my room at Wuthering Heights with the candle in… and the other candle is in Joseph's room. He's waiting for me to come home. There is the churchyard I must pass on my way. I won't lie in it alone, Heathcliff. I won't rest until you are lying in the grave next to me.'

I was looking for something to wrap around her to keep her warm when Mr Edgar came into the room.

'Oh, sir,' I said. 'Please help me. Mrs Linton is very ill.'

'Catherine, ill?' he said. 'Then shut the window, Nelly, and make the place warm.' He looked at his wife's white, haggard*

face and could not believe what he was seeing.

'Ah, you have come to see me, Edgar Linton. When I needed you, you didn't come. Now I don't need you, you are here. I am going to die, Edgar, and my resting place is out there near Wuthering Heights, not here with you.'

'Do you not love me any more?' he said. 'Do you love Heath—?'

'Hush!' cried Catherine. 'Mention that name again and I will jump from the window and kill myself. I don't want you any more, Edgar.'

'She is feverish*, sir,' I said. 'She does not know what she is saying.'

'I don't need your words, Nelly,' he said. 'You knew how ill she was but you did not tell me.'

I did not want to hear any more so I went out to fetch the doctor. On hearing my account* of Catherine's illness, he came with me. He made no secret of the fact that unless Catherine did as he told her she would die. Then he asked what had started the fever. At the sound of Heathcliff's name, the doctor told me something that made me shudder*.

A good friend of the doctor had seen Isabella and Heathcliff walking in the garden at the back of Thrushcross Grange for over two hours the previous night. Heathcliff was pleading with Isabella to get on his horse with him and leave. She put him off by saying she would do so next time they met.

The news filled me with fear. I ran back to the house and up to Isabella's room. She was not there. What could I do? It was too late to give chase and I could not upset Mr Edgar or Catherine any further, so I said nothing.

That night none of us slept, although for different reasons: Catherine, because of her fever; Mr Edgar, through worry for Catherine; me, for worrying about Isabella.

Early the next morning one of the maids came upstairs. 'Master, master!' she cried.

'What is the matter?' said Mr Edgar.

'Miss Isabella, she's gone! She's gone. Run off with Heathcliff!'

'That can't be true,' said Mr Edgar.

It was true. They had been seen at midnight heading away from the village. Mr Edgar said simply, 'I don't want to hear her name mentioned ever again.'

13 ∾ ISABELLA SENDS A LETTER

For the next two months Catherine was very ill. She had a brain fever*. Mr Edgar looked after her day and night. We all prayed she would get better, but the doctor said her brain would always be damaged. Yet there was some good news. She was pregnant! We all hoped she would have a son and heir*.

Heathcliff and Isabella were away for two months. Isabella wrote a short note to Mr Edgar saying she had married and was sorry for upsetting him. Mr Edgar never replied. A few weeks later I received a letter from her. It said:

Dear Nelly,

I came to Wuthering Heights last night and found out Catherine is very ill. I know I must not write to her or to Edgar so I am writing to you.

I would give anything to see Edgar again. From the day I left Thrushcross Grange I missed it. How much I want to come back now. But I can't!

Nelly, I must ask you two questions. How did you live at Wuthering Heights with all these strange people? They are not human. Secondly, and this I must know: Is Mr Heathcliff

40

a man? If so, is he mad? And if not, is he a devil? Tell me, Nelly, what have I married? You must come and see me, Nelly. Don't write but come and bring something from Edgar.

Now let me tell you about my welcome to Wuthering Heights. We arrived here yesterday in the dark. Heathcliff stayed outside to talk to Joseph. I went into the kitchen. What a dark untidy hole! By the fire stood a dirty-looking child with Catherine's eyes. It was Hareton. I went to shake hands and kiss him. He swore at me. I left and went across the yard and knocked on a door. It was opened by a tall thin man with long dirty hair. His eyes were deep set like Catherine's, but ghostly. It was Hindley Earnshaw.

'What do you want?' he asked.

'I was Isabella Linton,' I replied. 'I am now married to Mr Heathcliff.'

'He has kept his word and come back then,' he growled. 'Get in here,' he added.

As I stepped inside, he bolted the door.

'Could you show me to my room?' I asked.

He did not answer. For two hours, Nelly, I was locked in the room while he paced up and down. When I could stand it no longer, I asked him to get the maid so I could go to bed.

'We have no maid,' he said.

'Then where is my room?' I cried.

'Joseph will show you to Heathcliff's room. But remember to lock the door.'

'I do not want to lock myself in with Heathcliff,' I said.

Hindley pulled a gun from his waist. 'Every night I go up to his room and try the door. It is always locked. But, if one night I find it open, I will kill him. I swear I will kill him.'

'Why do you hate him so? Why don't you just tell him to leave your home?' I asked.

'It is no longer my house. He has taken it all from me and there is nothing left for Hareton. But I will get it all back and take his money too. And then I will kill him.'

He is clearly mad, Nelly. I was scared to be near him. I left and went back to the kitchen. Joseph was there, making porridge.

'I'll do that,' I said, taking the pot off him and pouring it into four dishes. Hareton ate like a pig and I could not bear to watch him. 'Show me to my bedroom,' I said to Joseph. He grumbled but took me upstairs to a tiny dark room.

'This is no place to sleep,' I said. 'Show me to Heathcliff's room.'

He took me down some steps and said nothing until we reached a door.

'This here is t'maister's*,' he said. 'But he always keeps it locked so you can't go in.'

I was too tired to argue. Joseph left me in the hallway. I eventually settled on a chair in Hareton's room.

I slept surprisingly well until Heathcliff woke me up. He asked why I was in the chair.

'Because you have the key to our room in your pocket,' I said.

'My room is not, and never will be, yours!' he screamed at me.

Oh Nelly, I hate him so much. I have been such a fool. Please come and see me soon. Please.

Isabella

14 ∾ NELLY VISITS WUTHERING HEIGHTS AND MEETS HEATHCLIFF

As soon as I read the letter, I told Mr Edgar. He should know Isabella wanted his forgiveness.

'Forgive her?' he shouted. 'I have nothing to forgive her for! Nelly, go and see her today and tell her I am not angry, just sorry to have lost her. But I cannot see her.'

'Will you write to her?' I asked.

'No,' he said. 'No, I will not.'

That afternoon I went to Wuthering Heights. As I walked up to the house, I could see her watching me through the window. I went straight in. What a dismal*, dreary* place, so different from when I was last there. Isabella looked thin and lifeless*. Her hair was untidy and dirty.

43

Hindley was nowhere to be seen, but Heathcliff was there. I had never seen him look better. He looked like the born and bred gentleman* that I knew he was not. Isabella came to me, holding out her hands. I shook my head. Heathcliff guessed what she was expecting.

'If you have brought something, give it to her,' he said.

'I have nothing to give,' I replied.

Isabella sat down shaking.

'How is Cathy?' Heathcliff asked.

I told him only the facts, making it clear that I thought she had brought her illness upon herself. 'She is getting better now but she will never be the same. If you really love her, you will not visit her.'

'Do you think I will leave her in Edgar's hands? Before you

44

leave you must promise me you will arrange for me to see her.'

'I will not. And you must not see her. A quarrel between you and Mr Edgar would kill her,' I said.

'Edgar does not love her like I do. He couldn't love her as much in eighty years as I could in one day. And Cathy loves me as much as I love her.'

'Catherine and Edgar are very fond of each other,' said Isabella.

'And Edgar likes you so much he doesn't even write,' snapped Heathcliff.

'That is because he does not know how I am feeling.'

'Sir,' I said, 'Isabella is unhappy. She is used to having a maid and being looked after. You must see what she has given up to be with you.'

'She left them because she thought I loved her,' he answered. 'And yet I never said such a thing. Now she knows I do not love her. That is why she is unhappy. She is a bigger fool than Edgar. She will be of use to me. That is why I am keeping her.'

'Mr Heathcliff,' I said, 'that is the talk of a madman.'

'Be careful what you are saying, Nelly,' said Isabella. 'He is a monster. He says he married me to get his revenge on Edgar. I do not know what his plan is but, whatever it is, I will stop him. Even if I have to die first.'

'Go to your room, Isabella!' he shouted, pushing her out of the door. Then turning to me, he said, 'You are not going yet, Nelly. I need your help to see Cathy. I swear I will not harm her. I just want to talk to her. I will wait every night at Thrushcross Grange until I see her.'

'It is so dangerous, sir,' I said. 'The surprise could kill her.'

I refused fifty times to do as he asked but in the end I agreed to take a letter to Catherine. I also promised to tell him when Edgar was away.

I did not know if I was right or wrong. I just hoped and prayed that this meeting would be their last.

15 ～ THE FINAL MEETING

Three days later I gave Catherine the letter. 'This is for you, Mrs Linton,' I said gently. 'Read it. He wants an answer now.'

She took it and read it with sadness in her eyes. Then she looked at me and pointed to the name.

'He is in the garden and wants to see you,' I said. 'What shall I tell him?' As I spoke I heard footsteps in the hall. It was Heathcliff. He came into the room and took her in his arms. They did not speak but held each other and kissed. He knew she was going to die soon. I could see it in his eyes.

'Oh, Cathy! Oh, my life! How can I bear it?' he said, staring hard at her.

Catherine looked at him. 'You and Edgar have broken my heart. I have no pity for you. You have killed me. I wish I could hold you until we are both dead. But you will live far longer than I. Will you forget me, Heathcliff, once I am gone?'

'You know I could never forget you. Don't hurt me so.'

'I do not wish you any more pain than I am feeling,' she said. 'My only wish is for us never to be apart.'

Heathcliff was so upset that he let her go and walked away. Turning to him, she said, 'Come to me, Heathcliff. You are my soul. I want to take you with me. I want to die at peace.'

She longed to hold him and managed to stand up. He turned and looked at her, his eyes wet. In a moment they were together, hugging and kissing. He held her so tight I feared for her safety.

'You have been so cruel to me, Cathy,' he said. 'You loved me more than anything. Nothing should have parted us and yet you chose to marry Edgar Linton. Why? I have not broken your heart

– you have broken it, and mine too. I do not want to live when you are dead.'

'You left me too,' she sobbed, 'but I forgive you. Please find it in your heart to forgive me.'

'It is hard to forgive, Cathy. I forgive you for hurting me but I cannot forgive you for dying,' he said, still holding her in his arms. She was silent. They just held each other with tears streaming down their faces.

'Mr Edgar will be back soon,' I said. 'You must leave.'

'No, no you must not!' she cried, holding him tightly. 'This will be our last time together.'

'I will stay then, my darling,' he whispered.

Mr Edgar came into the room and, on seeing them, went white with anger. Heathcliff calmly lifted Catherine and walked

across the room. He placed her in Mr Edgar's arms and walked out of the house.

16 ∾ THE BIRTH OF CATHERINE'S CHILD

Just after twelve o'clock that night, Catherine gave birth to a daughter. She too was called Catherine. She was the young lady you saw at Wuthering Heights, Mr Lockwood. Sadly, the effort of childbirth was too much for Catherine and she died two hours later.

Mr Edgar was devastated*. Not only had he lost his wife but she given him a daughter, not the son he longed for. Now, when he died, all his money would go to Isabella and her husband, Heathcliff.

That night was a long one. The baby cried and cried but no one cared. Mr Edgar simply sat staring into space. The whole house was in mourning*.

The next day Mr Edgar was sleeping, so I left Thrushcross Grange to go and find Heathcliff. I wanted to tell him Catherine had died but I did not know how I would break the news. I found him in the garden.

'Don't cry in front of me,' he snapped. 'I know she's dead. She doesn't want your tears.'

'Yes, she is dead,' I said.

'How did she die?' he asked shaking.

The poor man, I thought. He is grieving so much yet cannot show it.

'In her sleep,' I said.

'Did she ask for me?'

'Her senses never came back,' I said. 'She died in peace. I hope she wakes as peacefully in the other world*.'

'May she wake in torment*!' he cried. 'Catherine Earnshaw,

I pray you never rest in peace while I am alive. You said I killed you. Haunt me then! I know murderers are haunted. Haunt me until you drive me mad! I don't care. I cannot live without you!'

He banged his head against a tree and howled like a beast. His head and hands were covered in blood. 'Don't leave me. I cannot live without you!' he cried.

For several days Catherine's coffin lay in the drawing-room* at Thrushcross Grange. One night, when all were asleep, Heathcliff came to see her. Around her neck was a locket* containing a lock of Mr Edgar's hair. Heathcliff removed it and replaced it with one of his own.

The funeral took place on the Friday. Isabella was not invited. Hindley was, but did not come. Catherine was buried, not with the other Lintons or the Earnshaws, but in a corner of the churchyard nearest to the moors.

17 ∾ ISABELLA ESCAPES AND HINDLEY DIES

The next day was cold, wet, and dull. I was sat in the kitchen with baby Catherine, when a voice whispered, 'Nelly.'

I turned around to see Isabella standing there, soaking wet. She wore only a thin summer dress and slippers. There was a deep cut under her ear and her whole face was scratched and bruised.

'I have run away from Wuthering Heights,' she said. 'Please could you find me some dry clothes and I will be on my way.'

'You are not in a fit state* to go anywhere,' I said.

Only after I found her a coat and bathed her wound would she tell me what had happened.

'Nelly,' she said, 'I was so upset when I heard of Catherine's death.' As she spoke, she took off her wedding ring and threw it on the fire. 'I hate him so, I had to get away. He is evil. I wish I

could stay and look after Edgar and baby Catherine, but I know he will come for me. He is a monster. I did love him, Nelly, but he has destroyed me. I cannot forgive him.'

'How did you get away?' I said.

'Yesterday, Hindley, as you know, should have been at the funeral. The effort of staying sober* the night before was too much for him to bear. By dinner-time he was drunk and he locked all the doors. Heathcliff arrived home early and started banging on the front door. Hindley said he was going to kill him and took out his gun. Even though I hate Heathcliff, Nelly, I could not see him killed. I grabbed hold of Hindley's arm and shouted a warning to him.'

'What happened?' I asked.

'Heathcliff swore at me and told me to let him in. Hindley put his gun out of the window. He would have shot him but he was too late. Heathcliff grabbed it from him. The gun went off and at the same time Hindley's own knife slit his wrist. There was blood everywhere. Hindley fell down. Heathcliff jumped in through the window and began kicking and punching Hindley as he lay on the floor. I ran to get Joseph.

'The next morning, when I came down, Hindley looked terrible. Heathcliff just stood staring at the fire. His eyes were heavy and full of tears. Had it been anyone else I would have felt sorry for them, but not him. I took Hindley a glass of water and asked how he was feeling.

'"Not as ill as I wish," he said sadly, "but I am sore all over."

'I told him how Heathcliff had kicked him when he was senseless.

'"If only I had the strength to strangle him I would die happy," he said.

'"No," I said. "It is enough that he has murdered one of you."

'"What do you mean?" Hindley asked me.

'"Everyone knows Catherine would be alive now if it were not for Heathcliff. It is much better to be hated than to be loved by him."

'Hearing this, Heathcliff turned to me and shouted, "Get out of my sight."

'"I shall not," I said. "I loved Catherine and now her brother needs my help."

'"Get out before I kick you to death," he shouted.

'"Catherine would never have been happy as your wife," I shouted. He picked up a book and threw it at me. It hit me below the ear. I ran to the door. He came rushing towards me but Hindley stopped him. When I left, they were fighting on the floor.'

At this, Isabella stopped speaking. She stood up, kissed the portraits of Mr Edgar and Catherine, and went to her carriage. I have never seen her since, although she wrote to Mr Edgar regularly. She had a son called Linton. We tried to keep it quiet but Heathcliff found out from one of the servants. One day in the village he said to me, 'I hear I have a son, Nelly. You can tell Edgar Linton that one day he will be mine!'

Mr Edgar was a changed man after Catherine's death. He stayed mainly in the house and grounds of Thrushcross Grange. He never went anywhere except to visit her grave or to take long walks on the moors. He would not go anywhere there was a chance he might see or hear Heathcliff. In time he began to love baby Catherine, although he always called her Cathy, so she was never confused with her mother. It was his way of keeping them separate and yet, in a strange way, together in his heart and mind.

I often think, Mr Lockwood, of the different ways in which Mr Edgar and Mr Hindley reacted to the same situations. Both had been caring husbands, both loved their children, and yet when faced with tragic circumstances they reacted in different ways. Mr Hindley was much the weaker, taking to drink and letting himself go to ruin. Mr Edgar, on the other hand, showed real courage and loyalty to overcome his sorrow.

Mr Hindley died at the age of twenty-seven, six months after Catherine. How he died is a mystery, but he was drunk as a lord as usual. His death hurt me very deeply. I was far fonder of him than I was of Catherine. I had to know if he died naturally so I begged Edgar to let me go to Wuthering Heights, to make the final arrangements*.

I found out that Hindley had gambled away* all his money and Wuthering Heights itself. Heathcliff had everything and Hareton was left with nothing. I told Heathcliff that Hareton must come back with me, but he would not allow it. The poor boy had to stay and be a servant to his father's enemy in what should have been his own house.

18 ∾ CATHY VISITS WUTHERING HEIGHTS

The following twelve years were the happiest of my life. I had the job of bringing up Cathy. She was a most beautiful girl, with the Earnshaws' dark eyes and the Linton fair skin. She was a lively, sensitive*, and very loving child. In some ways she was the same as her mother, but not as intense*.

Mr Edgar had grown to love her very much. He never said a harsh word to her and took it upon himself to teach her. Cathy never left the grounds of Thrushcross Grange until she was thirteen. She knew nothing of Wuthering Heights or Heathcliff but sometimes she asked when she would be allowed to walk on the moors. She would look out of her window and ask about Penistone Crags which stood high on the moors. She often talked of seeing the view from them.

One day Isabella wrote to Mr Edgar to say that she was dying. She asked him to visit her and take her son, Linton, back to Thrushcross Grange with him. Mr Edgar went, as I knew he would. At first Cathy missed him terribly, but after a few days she began to ride alone in the grounds of Thrushcross Grange. I was not worried, as I thought she would not dare leave the grounds. How wrong I was!

One night she had not returned by tea-time and I was worried. I searched the grounds but there was no sign of her. In my heart, I knew that she had gone to Penistone Crags. I walked as fast as I could onto the moors until I reached Wuthering Heights. I knocked on the door. Zillah answered. 'Ah, you have come for Miss Cathy,' she said. 'I am glad you are not Heathcliff.'

'He is not in then?' I asked.

'No, he and Joseph are in the fields. Come in.'

Cathy was sitting in a chair talking away to Hareton, who was now a big lad of eighteen. He sat staring at her with his mouth open.

'Come home with me now!' I said to her. 'How dare you run off like that?'

Crying, she asked, 'What have I done? Papa will not mind. He never tells me off.'

I made her put on her hat and get ready to leave. She started to run around the room so that I could not catch her.

'If you knew whose house this is, you would be glad to leave,' I said.

'It's your father's, isn't it?' she said, turning to Hareton.

'No,' he said, looking away from her and blushing.

'Whose then?' she asked. 'Your master's? Who is your master?'

Hareton swore and turned away.

'Get my horse,' she said to Hareton, talking to him as if he was a servant. 'Get my horse now.'

'I will see you in hell first,' he said.

Cathy started crying. She turned to Zillah and said, 'You bring my pony.'

'Speak properly, Miss,' Zillah replied. 'Hareton, here, is your cousin and I am not your servant.'

'He is my cousin?' she laughed.

'Yes,' replied Zillah.

'It's not true. Papa has gone to London to get my cousin. He is a gentleman, not like this dirty urchin*.'

I was annoyed with Zillah and Cathy. Now Heathcliff would find out that Linton was coming to the Grange. Now Cathy would ask her father if she had a cousin at Wuthering Heights.

On the way home I told Cathy that, if her father ever found out about her visit to Wuthering Heights, I would lose my job. She promised never to tell him.

19 ∾ LINTON COMES TO THRUSHCROSS GRANGE

We had a letter from Mr Edgar to say that Isabella had died and he was returning home with Linton. Cathy was wild with excitement, not only at the thought of seeing her father but also of seeing her 'real' cousin.

Late into the afternoon, they arrived. Linton, who was only six months younger than Cathy, was asleep in the corner of the coach. He looked pale and sickly. Cathy wanted to play with him but Mr Edgar told her to leave him alone, as he was tired.

'Remember, Cathy,' said Mr Edgar, 'Linton's mother has just died and he is sad. He will not want to play just yet. This is your cousin Cathy, Linton,' Mr Edgar added, introducing* them.

Linton just wanted to lie down and Cathy fussed around him. Mr Edgar said how pleased he was that Linton was now at Thrushcross Grange.

Late that night, Joseph arrived at Thrushcross Grange. He wanted to see Mr Edgar.

'Heathcliff has sent me for his son,' he said, 'and I am not to go back without him.'

Mr Edgar was silent. He knew he could not keep Linton. He was not his own son: he was Heathcliff's.

Calmly, he said, 'Tell Mr Heathcliff that his son will come to Wuthering Heights tomorrow. He is too tired to come now.'

'I cannot go back without him,' repeated Joseph.

'You will not have him tonight,' Edgar said again.

'Very well!' shouted Joseph. 'If I don't take him, Heathcliff will come for him tomorrow.'

20 ∾ HEATHCLIFF WELCOMES HIS SON TO WUTHERING HEIGHTS

Early the next morning, Mr Edgar told me to take Linton to Wuthering Heights.

'When Cathy asks where he is, tell her his father sent for him and he had to leave us. Do not tell her where he has gone.'

I woke Linton and told him the news.

'My father?' he said. 'Mama never told me I had a father. I would rather stay here.'

'It is not far to Wuthering Heights,' I said. 'When you are stronger, you will be able to walk across the moors to see us.'

'Are Cathy and Uncle Edgar coming with me?' he asked.

'No, just me,' I answered.

'I will not go without Uncle Edgar,' he cried.

I had to promise him all sorts of things before he would leave. All the way across the moors he asked about his father and Wuthering Heights. He wanted to know why he had never seen his father and what he looked like.

It was only half past six when we arrived.

'Hello, Nelly!' cried Heathcliff, walking across to look at Linton.

'He looks just like a girl,' snarled* Joseph.

Heathcliff stared and then, laughing, said, 'What a beauty! He's worse than I expected!' Taking hold of the poor boy he added, 'You look just like your mother.' Linton looked at him, trembling.

'I hope you will be kind to him,' I said.

'I will be very kind to him,' he said, laughing. 'And to begin my kindness, Joseph, bring him some breakfast.'

I could stay no longer and left. The last words I heard, as I closed the door, were Linton shouting, 'Don't leave me! I'll not stay here, I'll not stay here.'

21 ∾ CATHY VISITS LINTON AT WUTHERING HEIGHTS

At first Cathy missed Linton, but she soon stopped asking about him. Whenever I saw Zillah in the village, I asked her how Linton was. 'I have never known such a soft creature,' she would reply. 'He always looks sickly and he is so selfish.'

Three years passed before Cathy saw Linton again. It was the day of her sixteenth birthday. Mr Edgar had said she could go up onto the moors with me to look at the grouse*. We set off together but she soon got ahead of me. I shouted for her to come back but it was too late. When I finally caught up with her she was with Heathcliff and Hareton.

'We must get back, Miss Cathy,' I said.

'Nonsense,' said Heathcliff. 'You must come back to Wuthering Heights and rest a while.'

'No,' I said, struggling to get her out of Heathcliff's grasp*. I was too late. Cathy was already on her way.

'You know she will see Linton,' I went on. 'I don't trust you. What are you up to?'

'I want her to see Linton,' he said. 'As to my plans, I want them to fall in love and marry. My son, Linton, will inherit all Edgar's wealth when he dies. So if Cathy marries him, she'll be rich. Of course, if Linton dies, then the money becomes mine. I am his only other living relative*.'

Cathy and Hareton had reached Wuthering Heights and were waiting for us. Heathcliff opened the door. I followed him. Linton stood by the fire. He had grown a lot since I had last seen him and he looked quite well.

'Linton, do you recognize your cousin?' Heathcliff asked.

'Linton!' exclaimed Cathy. 'Is it you? You are taller than I am!'

60

Linton walked towards her and she kissed him. They looked at one another, each unable to believe how the other had changed.

'You must be my uncle then,' cried Cathy. 'Why don't you visit Thrushcross Grange with Linton? All this time you have been so close and have never come to see us. Why?'

'Your father hates me because I married his sister, Isabella. He thought I was too poor for her and he has never forgiven me. If you tell him you want to come here, he will not let you.'

'Linton can come to see me,' she replied.

'I can't walk all that way,' said Linton. 'It would kill me!'

Heathcliff looked at him angrily and then, turning to me, said, 'How could anyone love such a selfish boy?'

Heathcliff stood up. He shouted for Hareton to come and show Cathy the animals. The two of them left and Heathcliff began to think aloud.

'I treat Hareton just as his father treated me. I send him to work in the fields and have given him no education. I know how he feels because it is how I felt. He is strong, clever, and handsome, but he does not know it. He is a rough farmhand* and this is how he will stay. And the best thing is – Hareton likes me!'

Linton stood up and went outside to join Cathy and Hareton. A few minutes later I could hear Cathy laughing. 'You can't read?' she mocked*.

Linton was giggling. 'He does not know his letters,' he said. 'What a dunce*, and he can't spell properly.' Hareton scratched his head. Cathy and Linton fell into fits of laughter. Rather than feel sorry for Linton, I began to dislike him.

It was late afternoon when we arrived back at Thrushcross Grange. We did not see Mr Edgar until the next day when Cathy, much to my anger, told him all about our visit to Wuthering Heights. Mr Edgar listened and then said, 'Why do you think I did not tell you where Linton was?'

'Because you dislike Heathcliff,' said Cathy.

'Not because I dislike Mr Heathcliff, but because he is the most evil man I know. He likes nothing more than to ruin people's lives. I knew that if you saw Linton you would see Heathcliff and he could ruin you.'

Mr Edgar told her of the way he treated Isabella and how he became the owner of Wuthering Heights. Cathy seemed to understand why her father did not want her to see Linton again.

That evening I found her crying. Linton was expecting to see her the next day. She wanted to write him a note but I told her she must have no contact with him.

Over the next few weeks, her behaviour changed. She would

write little notes and hide them. Each morning she got up early and waited in the kitchen. I found out that she and Linton had been writing love letters to each other. The letters were delivered by the milkboy.

When I told Cathy I knew about the letters, she was very angry. 'Don't tell papa!' she cried. 'Please burn them instead.'

'If I burn them, you must promise you will not contact him again,' I said.

'I promise, Nelly, but don't tell papa,' she pleaded*.

I burnt the letters and the next day sent a note to Linton telling him not to write or contact Cathy ever again.

22 ∾ ANOTHER BROKEN HEART

Cathy was very upset over the next few months. She had not seen Linton, and Mr Edgar became ill. He took fewer walks and spent less time with her.

One autumn afternoon we were walking in the garden and she started to cry. 'Oh, Nelly,' she said. 'What will I do when you and papa die? I will be all alone.'

'We have plenty of years left yet,' I said. 'Think how he would feel if he found out you loved Linton.'

'I love papa more than anything. I just want him to get better.'

'Fine words,' I said, 'but do you mean them?'

She did not answer and any further thoughts I had were stopped on seeing Heathcliff.

'Hello, Miss Linton!' he shouted.

'I do not want to talk to you. Papa and Nelly say you are wicked.'

'It is Linton I have come to tell you about. Two months ago you wrote love letters to him, then suddenly they stopped. Now he is ill. He is dying because of you. You have broken his heart.'

'How dare you tell such lies?' I shouted. 'Get out of here!'

He did not move except to turn to Cathy and say, 'I will be away for a month. Please go and see him. I swear he is dying.'

Cathy looked at him. I saw in her eyes that she had been fooled. I took her arm and marched her back to the house in silence.

Later that night I tried to tell Cathy that Heathcliff was lying. 'You may be right, Nelly,' she said, 'but I will not be at ease until I know.'

23 ∾ CATHY RETURNS TO WUTHERING HEIGHTS

It was a wet misty morning as Cathy and I made our way to Wuthering Heights. We went into the kitchen where Joseph sat. I asked if Heathcliff was in.

'Nay, nay!' he snarled. 'So go back where you came from.'

'Joseph!' cried a weak voice. 'Come and see to the fire at once.'

It was Linton. Cathy ran and kissed him as he lay on the sofa.

'Cathy, don't kiss me,' he said crossly. 'I can't breathe. And shut the door, it's so cold in here.'

'Well, Linton, are you glad to see me?' Cathy asked.

'Yes I am, but I am annoyed you did not come before. Papa said it was my fault and that you hated me. You don't, do you?'

'No, of course not,' she said. 'Next to papa and Nelly, I love you more than anyone else. But I can't come when Heathcliff is here.'

'Please come and see me again,' Linton pleaded.

'If I could get papa's permission I would spend half of my time with you.'

'My papa says you would love me more than your father if we were married,' said Linton.

'That is not true! I would never love anybody more than my own dear papa,' Cathy replied. Then she added, 'Sometimes people hate their wives, like your father hated Isabella.'

'Well, I'll tell you something. Your father hated your mother.'

'Oh!' said Cathy.

'Because your mother loved my father.'

'You liar! I hate you!'

'She did! She did!' cried Linton.

Cathy angrily pushed over the sofa. Linton fell backwards and started coughing so badly that it was ten minutes before he stopped. Cathy started to cry. She said she was sorry. She had not meant to hurt him.

'You have hurt me so much I will be awake all night,' he said, full of self-pity*.

'We must go,' I said.

Cathy looked slowly at Linton and then moved to the door. Linton fell to the floor, screaming. I knew he was acting but Cathy ran back. She took him in her arms and whispered something to him. I said we must leave.

'I hope you are not planning to go back to Wuthering Heights,' I said, as we made our way home.

'You can't stop me, Nelly,' she said.

'I will tell your father,' I said crossly. 'You must not see Linton again.'

'We'll see,' she replied angrily.

For the next three weeks I was ill. Cathy looked after both her father and me each day. In the evenings we both slept and so did not need her. I never thought about what she might be doing then, but I should have!

24 ~ CATHY SPENDS TIME WITH LINTON

One evening, when I was feeling better, I asked Cathy to read to me. She was not keen and kept making excuses. The next two evenings were the same. She was always looking at her watch and fretting*. I knew something was going on.

She said she had a headache and left me but, when I went to her room, she was not there. I looked out of the window to see her riding back across the moors. I waited for her return.

'Where have you been at this time of night?' I asked, knowing very well where she had been.

At first she lied, but slowly the truth came out. Every night while I was ill she had been seeing Linton. Most of the time she was unhappy with him. He was selfish and always moaning. She was only happy when he was in good spirits.

'We spent most of our time arguing,' she said. 'He wanted to laze around and I wanted us to do things together. Despite this, he begged me to return each evening. One night when I arrived Hareton was waiting for me.

'"Miss Cathy, I can read now," he said, starting to read the name "Hareton Earnshaw" that was above the door.

'I laughed at him when he couldn't read the numbers and he ran off. I went inside to see Linton. He was ill again. As I sat talking to him, Hareton burst into the room. He grabbed hold of Linton and told me to leave the room. Linton went white and trembled. I ran for Zillah, but when we returned Hareton had already taken Linton upstairs. I was told to leave.

'I did not go back for three nights in case he was dead. And I certainly did not want to see Hareton. When I arrived, Linton did not speak or look at me, so I left only to return the next night.

'"As you don't like me, Linton," I said, "this will be our last meeting."

'"Please sit down and stay a while," he said. "You are so much happier and nicer than I am. I feel so cross and bitter. But, Cathy, I love you and am truly sorry for the way I have treated you."

'I knew I had to forgive him, Nelly,' she said. 'We love each other.' Then, taking a deep breath, she added, 'I have told you everything now, Nelly. Nothing will stop me from going to Wuthering Heights. But please don't tell papa,' she pleaded.

As soon as she left, I went straight to Mr Edgar. The next morning he told Cathy that her visits were to stop.

25 ~ MR EDGAR ASKS FOR ADVICE

'All these things happened only a year ago, Mr Lockwood. I never thought I would be telling my story to a stranger to the family.'

'Please, Mrs Dean, I want to know what happened,' I said. 'Did Cathy obey her father?'

She did. She loved her father as he loved her. A few days later Mr Edgar asked me what I thought of Linton. I told him that he was not evil like his father and I felt that if they married, Cathy could control him. I added that he would have plenty of time to get to know his nephew* as he was far too young to marry yet.

Mr Edgar walked across to the window and sighed, 'I am not afraid of death, Nelly. I want to join Catherine. I know I have little time left. What shall I do about Cathy? Should I let her marry Linton? I will not mind if Heathcliff gains from the marriage so long as Linton is a good husband.'

'Let God decide,' I answered and left him to think.

Spring arrived and Mr Edgar was still ill. He wrote to Linton, asking to see him. Linton replied, saying his father would not allow him to visit. He asked that Mr Edgar come with Cathy to the moors where the three of them could talk. Mr Edgar could not agree to this request because he was far too ill to go with Cathy.

Linton sent many more letters. I have no doubt that Heathcliff helped him to write them. They pleaded with Edgar to let Linton see Cathy on the moors. It was not until June that he gave in. None of us had any idea how ill Linton was or how badly Heathcliff was treating him.

26 ❧ THE MEETING ON THE MOORS

It was a hot summer's day when Cathy and I set out to see Linton. We found him lying in the heather* close to Wuthering Heights. He looked pale and weak. Cathy spoke to him but he showed no interest. At last she said, 'If you don't speak to me, I might as well go home.'

'No! You can't,' he said. 'You must stay another half-hour.'

'But you would be more comfortable at home,' she replied. 'You look so ill.'

'Cathy, don't say I look ill, especially not to Heathcliff. If you see him, tell him I look well,' he pleaded.

'I will do no such thing,' Cathy replied.

'But he will get so angry,' Linton said.

'I don't care if he does.'

'But I do!' Linton shouted. 'He is an evil man.'

'Does he hurt you?' Cathy asked.

Linton did not answer. Cathy took his silence to mean he did not care for her any more.

'I must go now,' she said. 'I have been very disappointed with our meeting but I will come next week as you ask.'

We left Linton lying in the heather, waiting for his father.

27 ∾ PRISONERS AT WUTHERING HEIGHTS

Over the next few weeks Mr Edgar's health became worse. Cathy looked after him day and night, for she knew he was dying. She could not bear to leave him but I suggested she should visit Linton, as she needed the fresh air. Mr Edgar thought it would be good for Cathy. He did not realize that Heathcliff had had a hand in * Linton's letters.

Cathy and I rode across the moor to meet Linton. He was in the same spot as before. 'I didn't think you would come,' he said, looking frightened.

'Why don't you say you just don't want to see me?' cried Cathy. 'My father is ill and I should be at his side.'

Linton lay on the ground crying. 'Don't leave me, Cathy,' he sobbed. 'If you do, he will kill me! My life is in your hands. If you agree, he will not hurt me.'

'Agree to what?' she asked, taking him in her arms.

'I can't tell you. I dare not tell you.'

Linton cried and kissed Cathy's hands. I was wondering what the secret might be, when a voice called out, 'Nice to see you, Nelly.' It was Heathcliff. 'I hear Edgar is near death.'

'Yes,' I said sadly. 'It is true.'

'Linton is dying too,' Heathcliff said. 'I just hope Edgar goes first. Get up, Linton, and stop snivelling*.'

Linton tried but he could not move. Heathcliff walked across, grabbed him, and shouted, 'Get up, damn you!'

'I will, father,' he panted. 'I will do as you ask.'

'Walk with him, Cathy, will you?' Heathcliff asked. 'He hates me to touch him.'

'I can't go to Wuthering Heights,' Cathy whispered to Linton. 'You must tell me why you are so afraid.'

'Because I can't go into that house without you!'

'Stop!' Heathcliff shouted. 'If you won't go with him, I will take him myself.'

Linton pleaded with Cathy to go with him. She could not refuse, so we all walked to Wuthering Heights. On entering the house, Heathcliff immediately locked the door behind us. He turned to me and said, 'Hareton, Joseph, and Zillah are away. You will take tea?' Then he turned to Catherine and Linton. His mood changed. 'I hate you!' he snarled at them.

Cathy stood up and shouted, 'I am not scared of you! Give me that key.' She tried to take it from him but he tightened his grip.

'Get off or I will hit you!' he shouted.

Cathy took no notice. She grabbed his hand and bit hard. Heathcliff was shocked. He looked at me, then, taking hold of Cathy, hit her violently around the head several times. I ran at him but he pushed me away.

Cathy lay on the floor crying. Heathcliff turned to her and said, 'Cry as much as you like. In a few days I will be your father and I'll punish you like that as often as I like! Now, I am going to get your horses.'

My first thought, when he left, was to escape but he had locked all the doors and windows. I turned to Linton and pleaded with him to tell us his father's plan.

'Papa wants us to marry,' he said. 'And he wants it to happen now because he knows I am dying. You are to stay here all night. We are to be married in the morning. If you do as he says, he will let you return home and I shall come with you.'

'You are mad!' I shouted. 'You and your father have tricked us into coming here. You are wicked, evil people!'

'I'll burn the door down to get out of here,' shouted Cathy.

Linton started to cry. He felt sorry for himself. 'Cathy, my darling. My darling Cathy!' he wailed. 'You mustn't go. You must obey my father.'

At this point Heathcliff returned. On seeing Linton crying, he sent his son upstairs. Cathy pleaded with him to let us go home but he would not listen. He was enjoying the thought of her father's suffering. She begged him to let me go and tell Mr Edgar we were safe, but he refused that too.

'Your father will die thinking you have grown tired of looking after him and would rather spend your time with

Linton. How he must have hated you when you were born. I did. He gained a daughter but lost the woman he loved. And he will hate you when he dies.'

'I'll marry Linton now, if I can go home afterwards,' Cathy cried. 'How can I live if papa dies before I return?'

Heathcliff did not look at either of us. We were sent upstairs to Zillah's bedroom. Neither of us slept. Early the next morning Heathcliff took Cathy away. For five long days I was locked in the room, seeing nobody but my jailer*, Hareton.

28 ∾ ESCAPE FROM WUTHERING HEIGHTS

On the fifth morning Zillah came into the room. She looked relieved to see me.

'The whole village thinks you and Miss Cathy drowned in Blackhorse Marsh, but Heathcliff told me how he saved you.'

'Saved us!' I shouted. 'Saved us! We are his prisoners.'

I told Zillah what had happened and how we were tricked into coming to Wuthering Heights. When I finished, I grabbed my coat and ran past her. She did not try to stop me. I ran downstairs and into the kitchen. Linton lay on the settee*.

'Where is Cathy?' I demanded.

'Locked in her room,' he said calmly. 'She is now my wife and is not to go anywhere. No matter how ill she becomes, she is not to leave Wuthering Heights. Papa says she is just after my money.'

'Have you forgotten how kind she was to you last winter?' I asked. 'How can you believe your father's lies? You are a heartless*, selfish boy!'

'I can't stay in the same room as her,' he said crossly. 'She cries all night. I can't bear to hear it. Last night it was so bad I called my father and he said he would strangle her. It made no difference.'

'Where is Heathcliff?' I asked.

'Talking to the doctor. He says Edgar is dying. I am glad because then his fortune* will be mine and not Cathy's. Papa says Edgar's whole estate* will be mine. Yesterday she said she would give me all her books and her pony. I told her they were not hers to give, they were mine. She cried so I snatched a gold case from her neck. It had pictures of her mother and her father in it.'

'How could you be so cruel?' I said.

'She wouldn't let me have them. She pushed me away. I cried out and papa came rushing upstairs. When I told him what happened, he hit her in the face. Then he crushed the gold case with his foot and took away the picture of her mother.'

'How did you feel when he hurt her?' I asked.

'I didn't like all the blood. Now she won't speak to me, but father was right to punish her.'

I asked him for the key to Cathy's room but he refused, so I left before Heathcliff came back.

I arrived back at Thrushcross Grange to the amazement of all the servants. They thought I was dead. Edgar was very close to death. I told him what had happened, sparing him* some of the uglier details. Edgar knew Heathcliff was after his fortune through Linton. He asked me to send for a lawyer to ensure that if Linton died, Heathcliff would not get his money.

I sent four armed men to get Cathy and one unarmed man for the lawyer. The lawyer could not come until the next day and the four men returned without Cathy. I was furious.

At three o' clock that morning there was a knock at the door.

'Nelly. Nelly, is papa alive?'

It was Cathy. Linton had set her free.

'Yes. Yes he is!' I cried.

She went to see him and I waited outside. They talked calmly for fifteen minutes. Mr Edgar whispered, 'I am going to join

Catherine and you, darling child, shall come to us.' He never spoke or moved again.

Cathy sat dry-eyed with her father until dinner time when the lawyer came. He had been bribed* by Heathcliff to stay away. Now he told us Cathy and I would be allowed to stay at the Grange only until her father was buried.

29 ❧ HEATHCLIFF'S CONFESSION*

The evening after Mr Edgar's funeral, Cathy and I were talking, when Heathcliff burst in. He was the master now and could do as he wished. Cathy hurried to leave, but he grabbed her arm and said, 'Stop! Where would you run to? I have come to take you home to Wuthering Heights.'

Cathy knew there was nothing she could do. Turning to Heathcliff, she said, 'I shall come because I love Linton and he loves me. You have nobody. Nobody loves you and nobody will cry for you. You are evil!'

'Get your things!' he shouted.

Cathy left and he turned to look at the picture of her mother on the wall.

'I went to the churchyard yesterday, Nelly,' he said. 'I bribed the man who was digging Edgar's grave to open Catherine's coffin. She looked just the same. I could not stop looking at her. I broke open the side of her coffin away from Edgar's grave and bribed the man to bury me next to her when I die. He will take the side of my coffin away too, so I can hold her in my arms.'

'You are evil to disturb the dead,' I said.

'I disturbed nobody, Nelly. For eighteen years she has disturbed me night and day. Do you know, on the day she was buried I went to her grave. I wanted to hold her again. I dug down to her coffin and was about to take the lid off when I felt warm breath on my face. It was her! I was so happy. I knew she

was with me so I filled in the grave and ran back to Wuthering Heights. I rushed up to my room to see her. I could not see her but I could feel her.

'Since that night she has played plenty of tricks on me. I hear her outside my window, or in the room, or breathing on me. I open my eyes to look but she is never there! She is killing me. Slowly, she is driving me mad. Eighteen years I have had to put up with it.'

He was sweating. His eyes were fixed on Catherine's picture. I said nothing. Cathy entered, saying she was ready to go. She walked across to me and whispered, 'Goodbye, Nelly. Come and see me soon.'

'You will not, Nelly!' Heathcliff shouted, and with that they left. Cathy looked back at me with tears in her eyes.

30 ∾ CATHY IS STRANDED AT WUTHERING HEIGHTS

I have not seen Cathy since that day. I did visit the Heights once but Joseph would not let me in. Zillah, who I see in the village now and again, tells me what's going on.

When Cathy first arrived at Wuthering Heights she looked after Linton. He was dying, but Heathcliff refused to send for the doctor. 'I won't spend a penny on him!' he said. 'I do not care what happens to him.'

Linton died a few weeks later. Heathcliff took great delight in showing Cathy Linton's will. He left all he had to Heathcliff. I have no doubt Heathcliff forced him into doing so when he was ill. This left Cathy with no money and no friends. Zillah told me that she and Joseph have little to do with her. Hareton has tried to be friendly but she will have nothing to do with him because he is uneducated. She must be so unhappy.

I feel sorry for her, Mr Lockwood. I want to rent a cottage and ask her to live with me but I know Heathcliff would never allow it. Unless she marries again, she will always be a prisoner at Wuthering Heights.

And so ended Nelly Dean's story. I decided there and then I would not spend another winter at Thrushcross Grange. The very next day I would ride to Wuthering Heights and tell Heathcliff to find himself another tenant.

31 ✎ MR LOCKWOOD RETURNS TO WUTHERING HEIGHTS

It was a bright frosty morning as Wuthering Heights came into view. Hareton met me at the gate and took me inside. Cathy was in the kitchen. She did not even bother to look at me.

'She may be beautiful,' I thought, 'but she has no manners.'

I walked past her and, as I did so, dropped a note that Nelly had given me into her lap. I did not want Hareton to see it.

'What's this?' she said loudly.

'A letter from Nelly,' I whispered, hoping Hareton would not hear. But he did and snatched the letter from her.

'Mr Heathcliff will want to read this,' he said.

Cathy knew how to get what she wanted. She started crying and Hareton, not wanting to upset her, gave the note back. She read it eagerly*, and then asked me all sorts of questions.

'Nelly will want a reply,' I said. 'She always talks about you.'

'Tell her I cannot reply as I have nothing to write with. Nor do I have any books.'

'No books?' I cried.

'Heathcliff took them all away,' she said. 'They were my only pleasure and he took them away. I know some of them are in

80

Hareton's room. They are no use to him. He cannot read!' she shouted.

'Perhaps he wants to learn,' I said, trying to calm her down.

'Yes,' she laughed. 'I have heard him trying to read. It was very funny.'

Hareton, who was still in the room, blushed and left. Almost at once he was back, carrying a huge pile of books, which he threw into Cathy's lap.

'Take them!' he shouted.

'I will not!' she said. 'They will remind me of you!' She picked one up and started to read as Hareton would have read. He was angry and slapped her face. Then he picked up the pile of books and threw them on the fire. With that he stormed* out of the room.

Heathcliff arrived as Hareton left. He looked restless and glared at me.

'I have come to tell you I shall be leaving next week for London and do not intend to return for six months,' I said to him. 'I shan't want to rent Thrushcross Grange after October.'

My business done, I was ready to leave, but Heathcliff insisted I stay for lunch. He sent Cathy to the kitchen to dine with Joseph. So I sat down to eat with a grim*-looking Heathcliff on one side and the glum* Hareton on the other. As soon as we had finished I left, thinking the only way Cathy would be free would be for her to fall in love.

32 ∾ CATHY AND HARETON – 1802

I did not return to Yorkshire for several months. However, in early September I was visiting friends in the county when I found myself near Thrushcross Grange. As I was still paying rent, I decided to spend the night there.

The sun was setting when I arrived at the Grange to find Nelly had left and was now working at Wuthering Heights. I told the new housekeeper I was the tenant. She was to get a room ready for my return. I was going to Wuthering Heights.

It was nearly dark when I reached the Heights. There was a smell of fresh flowers and the doors were open. I heard talking.

'Read it again without any mistakes,' said a soft sweet voice.

The reader began. It was a male voice. I moved closer in order to see. He was a handsome young man. His hand followed the words across the page but every so often it would rise to touch the small, white hand on his shoulder.

This hand belonged to a young girl. She had lovely long brown hair and the most beautiful face. I thought, 'It is lucky he cannot see her face or he would not read so well.'

He finished reading without an error and received several kisses as a reward. Without seeing me, Cathy and Hareton stood up and left. I went into the kitchen to find Nelly. She was pleased to see me.

'Are you staying at Thrushcross Grange?' she asked.

'Only tonight and then I will be on my way. Why are you no longer at the Grange?' I asked.

'Zillah left and Heathcliff asked me to come,' she replied.

'Where is he?' I asked. 'I have come to settle up with him.'

'Oh, Heathcliff is dead, sir. He died three months ago.'

'Dead!' I said.

'Yes, sir.'

'Tell me. Tell me what happened,' I said.

'Well,' Nelly continued, 'two weeks after you left I came to work here for Cathy's sake. I wanted to try to make her life more bearable*. She was so unhappy. I managed to smuggle some books to her and for a while she felt better. She was very rude to Hareton at first. Then she began to realize she needed him as a friend. She changed her attitude and started to spend time with him, teaching him to read. They began to enjoy each other's company and finally fell in love. Oh, Mr Lockwood, I will be so happy when they marry!'

33 ∾ HEATHCLIFF FINDS OUT ABOUT CATHY AND HARETON

I asked what Heathcliff had thought of their love.

'He would have known nothing about it if it had not been for Joseph and his garden,' said Nelly. 'You see, Cathy persuaded Hareton to dig up Joseph's favourite fruit bushes so she could plant flowers. We were sitting quietly having lunch when Joseph rushed in, shaking with anger.'

'She's ruined my garden,' he shouted. 'I'll have to leave after sixty years. I can't stay here any longer. She's taken my garden from me and taken the boy's heart.'

'Is he drunk?' Heathcliff asked. 'What is he talking about, Hareton?'

'I pulled up a few fruit trees, that's all.'

'I asked him to do it,' said Cathy. 'I am to blame. I wanted to plant some flowers,' she added.

'Who said you could do such a thing?' Heathcliff shouted at Hareton. 'And who told you to obey her?'

Hareton was speechless*.

Cathy shouted, 'Why shouldn't I have a bit of garden? You have taken everything from me. My money! My land!'

'Shut up, you slut!' Heathcliff shouted.

84

'And Hareton's land and money!' she screamed. 'Hareton and I are friends now and I will tell him the truth about you!'

Heathcliff stood up as if to hit her.

'If you hit me, Hareton will hit you!' she cried. 'He won't do as you tell him any more.'

'Get her out of my sight!' thundered Heathcliff.

Hareton tried to move Cathy away but he was too late. Heathcliff stood up, grabbed hold of her hair, and pulled her head back. His eyes flashed. He was ready to tear her to pieces. But as he looked into her eyes, his anger disappeared and he let her go. He fell back into a chair, his hands covering his face. We all stared at him.

'You must not make me so angry,' he said. 'Nelly, take her away from me and if I see Hareton so much as look at her, I will send him away. Now get out of here, all of you!'

We left and soon Heathcliff went out, saying he would be back later.

When he returned, Cathy and Hareton were in the kitchen

reading. I was with them and happy to be so. They looked up at Heathcliff. He stopped, stared, and then turned away.

I don't know if you have ever noticed, Mr Lockwood, but their eyes are very similar. They are just like Catherine Earnshaw's. No wonder he could not look at the pair of them. He was looking into his Catherine's eyes.

Cathy and Hareton went outside, leaving me alone with Heathcliff.

'It is sad, Nelly,' he said. 'I have worked all my life to destroy the Earnshaws and the Lintons. I have all their money and land. Now I have it in my power to crush both of them and I don't want to. I couldn't hit Cathy earlier. Something strange is happening to me. I have to remember to eat and drink. I don't care about my daily life. I don't care if they spend time together. I don't want to speak about her, but she reminds me so much of my Cathy. I see her face everywhere I go. Every second of my life I am reminded that she was once here and I have lost her.'

'You are not ill, sir, are you?' I asked.

'No, Nelly,' he said.

'Then are you afraid of death?' I asked.

'No, I am not afraid of death, Nelly. But I can't carry on like this. I have to remind myself to breathe. I do not see anything other than my Cathy. I have one wish. My whole body and heart and brain have wanted it for so long. Oh God! It is a long fight. I wish it were over!'

34 ∾ HEATHCLIFF'S END

For the next few days he did not eat with us. Indeed, he ate very little. Then one night he left the house and did not return until the next morning. He looked different. Although he was pale and trembling, there was a sparkle in his eyes.

'You should not stop out all night, sir,' I said. 'You will catch a fever.'

'Leave me alone, Nelly,' he snapped back.

I was worried about him. Sometimes he would sit down as if to eat but then leave. He never looked at us but seemed to be looking at something we could not see. He would stare so intently*at it that he would often stop breathing.

'Where were you last night?' I asked.

'Last night, Nelly, I was on the threshold* of hell. Today I am in sight of heaven. I can see it. It is so close. But you had better go, Nelly, and then you won't see or hear anything to scare you.'

I took his advice and left. I did not see him until later that evening, when I took him his supper. He was staring into space. He told me to leave him alone. A little later I heard him going upstairs but he did not go into his room. He went into the room where you stayed, Mr Lockwood – Catherine Earnshaw's room. The one with the curtains around the bed. I could hear him above me, walking around, talking and crying all night long.

The following two nights were the same. He paced up and down the room, groaning and muttering. The only word I recognized was 'Catherine'. He spoke to her as if she were in the room with him.

On the fourth morning I managed to speak to him. 'You must eat and rest, Mr Heathcliff,' I said. 'You look ill. Your cheeks are hollow and your eyes red.'

'It is not my fault I cannot eat or sleep,' he replied. 'I will do both soon. I am so close to what I have always wanted. Only when I reach it, can I rest.'

He turned and looked at me with his deep black eyes. 'Nelly,' he said, 'I will die soon and when I do my coffin is to be carried to the churchyard in the evening. I have told you this before but I need to tell you again. Only you and Hareton will come with me. Make sure my orders, about how my coffin is to be placed, are obeyed. I want no ceremony* or Bible readings. I don't believe in that.'

Later that evening he went back to Catherine's room. All night long I could hear him moaning and groaning. I was so worried that I sent for the doctor, but Heathcliff refused to see him.

It rained throughout the night. Next morning, when I took my walk in the garden, I noticed his window open and the rain pouring in. 'He can't be in bed,' I thought. 'The rain would soak him. He must be up and about.'

I ran upstairs to the bedroom. The curtains around the bed were closed. I peeped through them. Heathcliff was lying on his back with his eyes open and a smile on his face. His clothes were soaking wet and yet he lay perfectly still. He was dead!

Quickly, I shut the window. I tried to close his eyes but they would not move! He lay with his lips slightly parted*, staring at me. I screamed for help.

A few days later we buried him as he had asked, next to Catherine. I hope he sleeps soundly but I doubt he will. The locals say his ghost can often be seen in the churchyard, or on the moors, and even at Wuthering Heights. I don't believe in ghosts, Mr Lockwood, but an odd thing happened to me a little while ago.

I was walking across the moors one dark evening when I met a little boy with some sheep. He was crying. I asked him what was the matter.

'Heathcliff and that woman are up there,' he said, pointing further up the moor and refusing to move.

I could see nothing, but neither the boy nor the sheep would go any further. From that day, I have never liked being out after dark or here at the Heights alone. I will be glad when Hareton

and Cathy are married and I can move with them to the Grange. Joseph will stay at Wuthering Heights but most of the rooms will be shut up. He will have no need of them and no one else will go there.

And so ended Mrs Dean's story. Soon after she finished I left Wuthering Heights, but on my way home I stopped at the churchyard. I soon found the three graves. Catherine's was in the middle, half covered with wild flowers. On one side lay Edgar's, covered only in turf*, and on the other side, Heathcliff's, still a mound of bare earth. I stood listening to the soft wind and watching the butterflies. It was a calm and restful scene. How could anyone imagine that these three souls were not at peace, at last?

GLOSSARY

3 **bleak** empty, bare, unfriendly
   moors an area of rough, wild
   countryside with few trees
   deformed changed in shape
   tenant a person who rents a
   property (pays money to its
   owner in order to live there)
   stables buildings where horses
   are kept

4 **cellar** an underground room
   where wine is often kept
   housekeeper a person employed
   to look after a house

5 **taken… by** interested in
   t'field Yorkshire dialect for 'the
   field'
   t'missis Yorkshire dialect for 'the
   mistress' (the woman who is in
   charge of a house)

7 **clothes press** cupboard with
   shelves for clothes

8 **Terrified** very frightened
   wailed cried loudly

9 **grinding his teeth** pressing teeth
   hard against each other in anger

10 **wrenched** pulled
   At first light when the sun
   first rose
   let rent out; allow someone to
   live in your property in return
   for money
   widow woman whose husband
   has died

12 **ragged** untidy looking, not
   cared for

13 **lass** girl

14 **name** good reputation

15 **lantern** a lamp for carrying with
   a candle inside

17 **wicked** bad, evil
   admired thought well of
   so superior to so much better
   than
   flog beat, hit
   flattering saying nice things
   about someone (so that they
   will like you)

18 **black** dirty
   accepted agreed to (the
   invitation)

19 **be jealous of** distrust
   broad wide
   rascal naughty person

20 **revenge** get somebody back for
   what they have done

21 **rarely** not often
   headstrong stubborn, wanting
   her own way
   in a black mood very angry and
   unhappy
   affection love and kindness

22 **frock** dress

24 **courtyard** a yard with walls
   round it
   could not resist had to
   quarrel argument

banister handrail beside the stairs

25 **barn** a large building on a farm where animals or crops are kept

26 **degrade me** make me less important than I am now

29 **eternal** everlasting

30 **fondness** liking, kindness
short direct, a little rude
impatiently wanting things to happen quickly

31 **hesitated** stopped for a moment

32 **plotting** planning

34 **borrowed money on his land** used the value of his land as a guarantee for a loan (and so risked losing his land)
bonnet a hat with strings that tie under the chin

37 **ramble** talk without making sense

38 **haggard** worn-out looking

39 **feverish** ill, with a high temperature and fever
account story
shudder shiver

40 **brain fever** illness affecting the brain
heir person who will gain someone's property when they die

43 **t'maister's** Yorkshire dialect for 'the master's'
dismal grey

dreary dull
lifeless lacking energy

44 **born and bred gentleman** gentleman by birth (his family) and upbringing

49 **devastated** very upset
mourning great sadness because of somone's death
the other world heaven
torment suffering

50 **drawing-room** a large sitting-room where guests are greeted
locket small case worn around the neck on a chain; often holds a picture
not in a fit state not well enough

51 **sober** not drunk

54 **final arrangements** funeral arrangements
gambled away lost money by gambling (risking money on games of chance)
sensitive aware of the feelings of others
intense having strong feelings

57 **urchin** a scruffy boy
introducing giving names on meeting

59 **snarled** said angrily

60 **grouse** bird found on the moors
grasp grip
relative family member

62 **farmhand** worker on a farm
mocked teased
dunce idiot

63 **pleaded** begged

65 **self-pity** feeling sorry for oneself

67 **fretting** worrying

69 **nephew** brother's or (in this case) sister's son
heather plant found on moors, with small purple flowers

71 **had a hand in** helped to write

72 **snivelling** crying and sniffing

75 **jailer** person who looks after prisoners
settee sofa
heartless not caring about the feelings of others

76 **fortune** wealth
estate land and all possessions
sparing him leaving out (because they might cause pain)

77 **bribed** paid money to make him do something
confession when somebody admits what they have done

80 **eagerly** keenly; with great desire

81 **stormed** rushed angrily

82 **grim** serious, harsh
glum unhappy looking

84 **more bearable** easier
speechless lost for words

87 **intently** closely; with all his energy
threshold edge

88 **ceremony** formal religious service
parted open, apart

90 **turf** grass-covered earth